Reading Essentials
in Social Studies

AMERICA AT WAR!

To Jesse A. Alderson,

Washington Is Burning!

Your friend,

The War of 1812

Alvin Robert Cunningham

Alvin Robert Cunningham

PERFECTION LEARNING®

To the loving memory of my late mother, Lorene Cunningham, and younger brother, Pete Cunningham

Editorial Director: Susan C. Thies
Editor: Mary L. Bush

Cover Design: Michael A. Aspengren
Book Design: Emily J. Greazel, Deborah Lea Bell, Tobi Cunningham
Image Research: Lisa Lorimor, Emily J. Greazel

Photo Credits:
© CORBIS: pp. 16, 29 (top), 36–37; North Wind Pictures:
pp. 4 (top), 14, 20–21, 23 (bottom), 27, 30, 31, 34 (bottom), 36,
42–43, 43

ArtToday (some images copyright www.arttoday.com): cover, pp. 1, 2,
2–3, 4 (background), 4 (bottom), 9, 10, 10–11, 12 (background),
13 (top), 14 (background), 17, 18, 18–19, 19, 20, 22, 23 (top),
25 (center and bottom), 26 (top), 28, 29 (bottom), 34 (top), 35, 39,
40, 41; Library of Congress: 4–5, 6–7, 8, 11, 12, 15, 26 (bottom),
32–33, 37, 44, 45

For information, contact
Perfection Learning® Corporation
1000 North Second Avenue, P.O. Box 500
Logan, Iowa 51546-0500.
Phone: 1-800-831-4190 • Fax: 1-800-543-2745
perfectionlearning.com

1 2 3 4 5 BA 06 05 04 03 02

ISBN 0-7891-5896-5

Contents

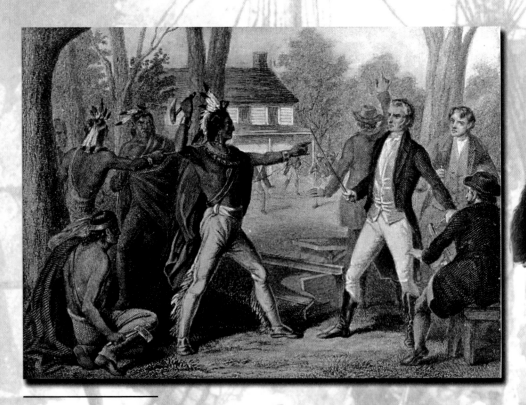

Tecumseh fighting
against the Americans
at Fort Meigs

Napoleon Bonaparte

Tecumseh

Introduction

MANY historians refer to the War of 1812 as America's second war for independence. This war tried to settle arguments between the United States and Great Britain that had been going on since the end of the American Revolution in 1783.

Canadian Conflicts

The United States was irritated by Britain's failure to remove its forces from the American forts and lands along the Great Lakes. Why couldn't these troops just cross the border into Canada, which was a British **colony** at that time?

Many Americans also blamed the British and the Canadians for encouraging Indians to attack the settlers on the **frontier**. The Shawnee Chief Tecumseh tried to establish an Indian **alliance** of northern and southern Indian nations. He wanted to make this alliance powerful enough to stop the American settlers from moving into Indian lands. When the War of 1812 broke out, Chief Tecumseh and some tribes in his alliance fought with the British and Canadians against the United States.

The Napoleonic Wars

By 1812, Great Britain had been fighting France for many years. The French ruler at the time was Napoleon Bonaparte, so these conflicts became known as the Napoleonic Wars. Eventually France controlled much of Europe, while Great Britain controlled the seas.

Being a **neutral** country at this time brought great prosperity for the United States. Products were grown or manufactured and then shipped and sold to the warring countries.

Over time, however, British **maritime** policies damaged American business. The British Orders in Council declared that all neutral shipping had to be channeled through Great Britain first. There, the British could stop goods from going to France.

Once an Englishman, Always an Englishman?

Impressment was another Orders in Council policy that angered Americans. This was Britain's practice of boarding U.S. ships to haul off American sailors who had been born in Britain. British naval officers insisted, "Once an Englishman, always an Englishman." During this time, many American-born sailors were taken by mistake.

This crisis came to a head when the U.S. **frigate** *Chesapeake* refused to be searched. As a result, the British ship *Leopard* opened fire, killing three Americans and wounding eighteen others.

This caused President Thomas Jefferson and Congress to pass the Embargo Act of 1807. The act made it illegal for American

Orders in Council

The British Orders in Council were orders from the king or queen, and they had the power of laws. Orders were usually created when the country faced serious problems. The king or queen relied on the advice of a council, or group of advisors, to help make his or her decision.

ships to trade with foreign countries. It was intended to hurt the British but ended up devastating Americans. The New England shipping business almost came to a halt, and Southern farmers had no one to sell their products to.

Declaration of War

The American people were split on the war issue. Most New Englanders were opposed to the war since it would hurt their businesses even more. One group of congressmen called the War Hawks were in favor of going to war. They pressured the president and Congress to declare war on Great Britain. Finally, on June 18, 1812, President Madison asked Congress for a declaration of war.

Unknown to Americans at the time, Great Britain had suspended the Orders in Council policies two days before this vote. If the United States had received the message in time, there might never have been a war.

The War of 1812

When the War of 1812 began, the United States was unprepared. The country's army was small and scattered around the frontier. The undisciplined **militia** tried to support this army. The American navy had only six warships. Great Britain was one of the mightiest nations in the world with 116 warships.

America lacked any real military leadership and endured many losses at first. It also suffered the humiliation of having its new capital city burned by British soldiers. President James Madison and his **cabinet** were forced to flee to the countryside for safety.

The war lasted from June 18, 1812, to February 16, 1815. Representatives of both countries actually signed the Peace Treaty of Ghent at Ghent, Belgium, on December 24, 1814. But in those days, it took many weeks for messages to cross the Atlantic Ocean. So it wasn't until February 16, 1815, that the U.S. Senate approved the treaty and President Madison signed it into law.

In the meantime, the Battle of New Orleans took place nine days after the peace treaty had been signed. Both sides lost lives in this battle, which wouldn't have taken place had news of the treaty reached the United States faster. So, like its beginning, the end of the War of 1812 would likely have been different had there been quicker communication between the two countries.

❖ ❖ ❖ ❖ ❖ ❖ ❖ ❖ ❖ ❖ ❖

The historical fiction chapters of this book tell the story of Sophie Turner, one of President Madison's black slaves. In her desire for freedom, this teenager helped First Lady Dolley Madison save a portrait of George Washington before the British burned the President's House.

James Madison

The nonfiction chapters discuss the important events leading up to and following the burning of Washington, D.C. The lives of James and Dolley Madison and their relationship to the war are explained. Insights into the role that black Americans played in the war are also provided.

President's House

The original name for the house that the president and his family lived in was the President's House. Throughout the 1800s, however, it was nicknamed the "White House" because of the **whitewash** used to cover the cracked stone on the outside. A vote from Congress made the name official in 1902.

Worth the Fight

"Let's just escape from this house and run to the British soldiers, Pa," cried Sophie Turner. Tears streamed down her cheeks. "We can at least be *free* with them!"

Cyrus Turner put his arm around his teenage daughter. "I can't do that, Sophie," he said. "I'm an American, and I'm going with Mr. Madison to Bladensburg to fight with the militia."

Mr. Turner put the **powder horn** over his shoulder. "We have to stop the British from reaching Washington."

"But, Pa," Sophie argued, "you're just one of President Madison's slaves. You're not a real American!"

Mr. Turner looked down at his daughter with hurt in his eyes.

"You could be wounded or killed!" exclaimed Sophie. "What would I do then?"

"I'll be coming back," he said softly. "Besides, Mr. Madison is a good president and a kind master. He might just give me my freedom if I fight for our country."

Sophie wiped the tears from her eyes.

"Let's just think about all the good things we have," said Sophie's father. "We have our black brothers and sisters at the Madisons' Montpelier home. They aren't whipped or beaten like on other plantations. Mr. Madison sees to that. And our families have been kept together for generations."

Slaves planting rice on a plantation

Sophie watched her father pick up the long **flintlock musket**. Mr. Turner looked into his daughter's eyes.

"We live in the President's House," he continued. "Your Aunt Tillie is Lady Madison's personal servant. You are now a housemaid in this beautiful mansion. Aunt Tillie has even taught you to read and write some."

Mr. Turner put on his **tricorn**.

"And I am the president's gardener." He smiled as he spoke. "So our lives could be a lot worse."

"But they *are* a lot worse, Pa!" Anger gnawed at Sophie's insides. "We aren't free! We're just slaves! Most people think of us as property!"

Mr. Turner took his daughter's hand and led her to a large painting. It was a portrait of George Washington. Sophie had dusted it many times.

"When I look at our first president," he said, "I see George Washington with a black face. He stands for all the black soldiers who fought the British for our country's freedom and their own."

"But, Pa—"

"Listen, Sophie," her father said. "Did you know that Washington freed his 300 slaves? It was in his will."

Her father's words made Sophie examine the painting more closely.

"Look, he has his left hand on his sword," her father pointed out. "I believe his right hand is inviting me to fight for my freedom."

Sophie looked at her father.

"This morning, I prayed to this painting to help keep me safe in battle," Mr. Turner said. "I asked it to help us defeat the British a second time and give me freedom when the war is over."

Sophie hoped her father's prayers would be answered.

President Madison in Chains!

Sophie stared at the painting of Washington. She thought about the conversation with her father two days earlier. Shortly thereafter, he had left with Mr. Madison to find General Winder's militia. Everyone was hoping for an American victory at Bladensburg.

"Sophie? Sophie!"

The memory evaporated. Sophie turned to face Aunt Tillie and Lady Madison.

"Sophie," said Mrs. Madison, "Yesterday a messenger brought me some bad news. The enemy's forces are stronger than reported. Mr. Madison has asked me to pack some trunks with important cabinet papers."

"Why?" asked Sophie.

"To protect them from the British if they defeat our forces and invade Washington."

Sophie saw the worry in Mrs. Madison's eyes.

"Yesterday we filled four trunks with the papers," explained Aunt Tillie. "Now I need your help putting them into the carriage."

"Any word from Pa?"

"No," answered Mrs. Madison. "But since sunrise, I've been looking out an upstairs window with my **spyglass**."

"What did you see?" asked Sophie.

"Groups of military are wandering around the streets," said Mrs. Madison. "They seem to be preparing for something. I'm concerned about my husband's safety."

"Don't worry," said Aunt Tillie. "Nothing's going to happen to President Madison."

"But we've heard that the British want to capture him and put him in chains!" Mrs. Madison cried.

Sophie watched her aunt put an arm around her **mistress**.

"Then they plan to lead him through the streets of London!" Mrs. Madison shook her head. "It's too horrible to even think about!"

Sophie bit her lip. What about the black slaves she'd seen chained and led through the streets of Washington? she thought. Did anyone find *that* too horrible to think about? Why should President Madison in chains be any different?

Silently, Sophie followed the two women to the president's office. There, she and Aunt Tillie picked up one of the trunks and carried it outside. Mrs. Madison followed.

When Sophie reached the carriage, she stopped and looked around. "What happened to all the soldiers?"

The first lady looked surprised.

"They left a long time ago," said the black carriage driver. "They just sneaked away like thieves in the night."

"All 100 of them?" asked Mrs. Madison.

"Well, mistress, I guess they were just trying to save their own skin," answered the driver. "Might be a good idea if everyone in the President's House does the same thing before the British arrive."

"I'm confident our American forces will be victorious at Bladensburg," said Mrs. Madison. "After your carriage is loaded, my house servants will prepare the usual 3:00 dinner. Today it will be a special victory dinner for my husband, his cabinet, and the military officers."

First Females

The wife of a president is called the *first lady*.

After Sophie finished loading the trunks, she helped prepare the celebration dinner. She set the table and brought in the **ale**, cider, and wine. Placing the drinks in the coolers, she glanced at Mrs. Madison. The first lady's eyes were filled with worry.

At 3:00 p.m., the dining room was ready for the victory celebration, but no one had returned from Bladensburg yet.

Now Sophie started to worry. She walked over to the Washington painting. Quietly, she repeated her father's prayer to the president.

White House dining room

For All the Black Soldiers

"Lady Madison! Lady Madison!" shouted French John, the supervisor of the household servants. "It's a messenger from Bladensburg!"

Sophie stopped praying. She and the other slaves followed the first lady to the front entrance. Sophie stopped next to Aunt Tillie.

"Clear out! Everyone clear out *now*!" shouted the dusty soldier. "Our militia's been defeated by the British. Wounded and dead soldiers cover the battlefield!"

The young man had to stop and catch his breath before continuing. "Some militia stayed and are making a brave stand with Commodore Barney's sailors and their cannons. But they can't hold back the British **regulars** for long!"

Sophie felt her aunt's arm around her. She hoped that her father was not one of the wounded or killed.

"What about my husband and his men?" asked the first lady.

"They were still at the battlefield when I left," answered the messenger. "The president said you were to leave immediately and seek a place of safety. It's just a matter of time before the British invade Washington."

Sophie glanced toward the dining room. The china plates, silver **goblets**, bowls of food, and bottles of wine would never be part of a victory celebration.

The messenger was still speaking, so Sophie turned back and listened.

"I was ordered to warn all the people I see to hide in the countryside or in their homes. The **refugees** have taken all the available wagons in Washington. The president hopes that the British will not harm any of the stranded **civilians**."

The messenger bowed slightly and rushed away. Lady Madison turned to her handful of servants. She told her **coachman** to fetch her sister and brother-in-law and park the carriage in front of the mansion. Then she told French John to take all the slaves, except Tillie and Sophie, and hide them in his basement.

Sophie and her aunt watched the others leave.

Sophie turned to Aunt Tillie. "It has to be saved," she whispered.

"What?" Aunt Tillie asked.

"The Washington portrait on the dining room wall."

"What are you talking about, Sophie?" whispered Aunt Tillie.

"It's the painting that Pa prayed to before he left to fight," whispered Sophie. "If it's safe, then Pa's safe."

"Stop talking nonsense, girl!" ordered Aunt Tillie.

But Sophie ignored her aunt and walked straight over to Mrs. Madison. "We can't leave that painting of George Washington for the British to destroy!" she announced.

The first lady looked at the portrait and then at the young housemaid.

"Isn't he the father of this city—of this country?" Sophie argued. She didn't want to tell Mrs. Madison the real reason she wanted the portrait saved.

Just then, two New York friends of the first lady opened the front door. "Anything we can help you with, Dolley?" one of the men asked.

"We have a wagon outside," said the other.

"Yes," Mrs. Madison replied. "I want that painting of Washington saved. Break the glass case and cut it out."

The three females watched the two men complete the task.

"Now take it to a safe place," Mrs. Madison ordered. "And don't let it fall into the hands of the British!"

Cyrus Turner's smiling face appeared in his daughter's mind. "It's for all the black soldiers, Pa," she whispered.

The Battle of New Orleans. Black soldiers played an important role in this battle.

Freedom Tears

The next morning, Sophie awoke in her clothes from the day before. She rubbed her eyes and tried to clear her head. The events of the previous day came back to her.

Mrs. Madison had made plans to travel to Rockeby, a country mansion about ten miles into Virginia. The house belonged to a friend of the first lady. Other refugees from Washington would be staying there as well.

Sophie had ridden in a crowded carriage. She was on one side with Aunt Tillie and Charles Carroll, a friend of the president. Mrs. Madison, her sister Anna, and her brother-in-law Richard Cutts were on the other side. Mr. Cutts was Washington's superintendent general of military supplies.

Mrs. Madison's carriage had first stopped at the home of Navy Secretary Jones. Having received word of the complete defeat at Bladensburg, the secretary agreed that the first lady should cross into Virginia and find safety.

The carriage ride to Rockeby had been slow and difficult. The dark road was jammed with refugees. Most walked next to their wagons, which were stacked high with their household furniture. Sophie had noticed the black slaves walking behind their masters. Each was carrying some personal item. Fear was in their eyes.

✵ ✵ ✵ ✵ ✵ ✵ ✵ ✵ ✵ ✵

"Sophie," Aunt Tillie called. "Sophie!"
Sophie snapped back to the present.

"What, Aunt Tillie?"

"Come here, girl," said Aunt Tillie, pointing to the window. "Look at what the British have done to our city!"

Still groggy from sleep, Sophie walked slowly to the window. "The sky is red—what time is it?"

"It's early in the morning, Sophie, and that's fire."

"Fire?" said Sophie. "What's burning?"

"Our city," answered Aunt Tillie. "The British are burning our city."

Sophie Turner tried to understand the scene before her. "Washington is burning?" she mumbled to herself. Quickly, her eyes and mind completely cleared, and she understood what was happening. "Washington is burning!" she exclaimed.

Sophie turned and looked at her aunt. "What about Pa?" she asked.

"Your father is all right," Aunt Tillie replied.

"How do you know?" asked Sophie.

"A messenger came last night when you were asleep," explained Aunt Tillie. "When the militia ran from the battlefield at Bladensburg, your father stayed and fought with Commodore Barney's troops. Your father, the commodore, and many of his sailors were wounded and taken prisoner."

Wounded? Taken prisoner? The words scared Sophie.

"But the British general **paroled** them all for their bravery," continued Aunt Tillie.

"Where's Pa now?" asked Sophie.

"The soldiers were all taken to Bladensburg to get their wounds treated," explained Aunt Tillie. "Soon they'll be home."

Sophie walked back to the window and stared at the red glow above Washington. She knew in her heart that her father's prayer would somehow be answered. Someday he and all black citizens would be freed. After all, once America regained its freedom, it would have to free its slaves, wouldn't it?

Sophie started crying as she thought of all the free black soldiers. As she watched Washington burn, tears of freedom ran down her face.

Battles Around the Great Lakes

1812–1813

At the beginning of the war, the American War Hawks pushed to invade and conquer Canada, which was a British colony at the time. With the British involved in the Napoleonic Wars, the War Hawks felt this would be an easy undertaking. Then Canada would become part of the United States, and America would not have to worry about future British invasions from the north.

Battle of Lake Erie

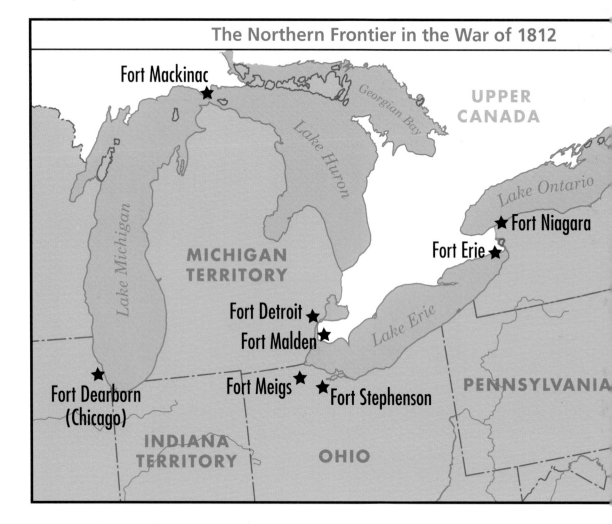

The Northern Frontier in the War of 1812

Fort Mackinac
UPPER CANADA
Georgian Bay
Lake Huron
Lake Ontario
Fort Niagara
Lake Michigan
Fort Erie
MICHIGAN TERRITORY
Fort Detroit
Fort Malden
Lake Erie
Fort Meigs
Fort Stephenson
PENNSYLVANIA
Fort Dearborn (Chicago)
INDIANA TERRITORY
OHIO

Early Defeats

In the first period of the war, most of the fighting took place between the western end of Lake Ontario and the western end of Lake Erie. The battleground was between Fort Niagara and Fort Detroit. This land war got off to a very bad start.

The British attacked first. General Isaac Brock led a mixed force of Canadians, British, and Indians across the Detroit River to Fort Malden. After a short **siege**, American General Isaac Hull hoisted a white flag of surrender.

About that same time, Fort Mackinac fell to the British. On orders from General Hull, Fort Dearborn was abandoned. American forces were also defeated at Fort Niagara.

NEW YORK

A Famous Past

Fort Dearborn was located in the area that is now Chicago, Illinois.

These early failures showed the American people the price of going to war without properly trained soldiers and leaders.

Early Victories

The American navy was more successful than the land forces, especially in one-to-one battles. The navy was able to score a few key victories by sea.

In order to regain the city of Detroit, Americans knew they had to take control of Lake Erie. Captain Oliver Hazard Perry was ordered to build a **fleet** that would defeat the British. In the Battle of Lake Erie, Perry's forces severely damaged two British ships, causing the entire fleet to surrender.

On April 22, 1813, American General Henry Dearborn sailed his forces to Upper Canada's capital of York (now Toronto). When advancing through the fort, a powder magazine, or mine, exploded. Many British and Americans were killed. This resulted in many American soldiers **looting** and burning the public buildings of York. The British would later get their revenge with the burning of Washington.

Oliver Hazard Perry

Henry Dearborn

With Lake Erie under American control, General William Henry Harrison's army sailed for Fort Malden in Canadian Territory. Faced with this threat, the British abandoned both Fort Malden and Detroit. But American forces caught up with them at the Thames River. They defeated about 900 British regulars and 2,000 Indians. The famous Chief Tecumseh was killed in this battle.

William Henry Harrison

The American forces were led by Colonel Richard M. Johnson at the Battle of Thames.

1814

After the attack on Washington, D.C., the British were ready to launch their big land and water attack along Lake Champlain. About 10,000 British advanced into the United States from Montreal. They thought only a weak American force stood between them and New York City. But on September 11, 1814, American Captain Thomas Macdonough won the naval battle of Lake Champlain (Plattsburg Bay), destroying the British fleet. The British army retreated into Canada.

Thomas Macdonough

A SLICE OF **BLACK HISTORY**

- The majority of blacks who fought in the War of 1812 were slaves, but some were free blacks. Free blacks were ex-slaves who had earned or bought their own freedom or had been set free in their masters' wills.

- Blacks soldiers proved to be a valuable resource in naval battles of the War of 1812.

- When Commodore Perry won his great victory on Lake Erie, at least one out of every ten sailors on his ship was black. Perry spoke of his black crew members as "absolutely insensitive to danger."

- Commodore Thomas Macdonough reported that the accuracy of his black gunners was responsible for his victory on Lake Champlain.

The Invasion of Washington

The overthrow of Napoleon Bonaparte of France in 1814 was an important turning point in the war. The British government was now free to make a stronger effort to conquer the United States. It was able to send about 15,000 more troops across the Atlantic to help crush the United States and end the war. Having recently defeated Napoleon, the British were very confident that they could destroy the much weaker Americans.

Protecting Washington?

John Armstrong

William Winder

Despite hearing that a powerful **squadron** with about 4,000 redcoats had been raiding the eastern coast, Washington stayed practically defenseless. President Madison had listened to Secretary of War John Armstrong who was convinced that the British would not attack Washington. But by July 1814, President James Madison had placed General William Winder in charge of the Potomac Military District. Winder would command the land forces, which were mostly militia troops.

Madison also placed Commodore Joshua Barney in charge of naval defenses. This amounted to just three gunboats, some **barges** with mounted cannons, and about 500 sailors.

Battle of Bladensburg

In August 1814, a British fleet under the command of Admiral George Cockburn sailed up the Patuxent River. At Benedict, Maryland, the fleet unloaded about 4,000 British troops and their leader General Robert Ross. This British force then started a 45-mile march toward Washington.

The Americans had destroyed the two bridges entering Washington from the east across the Potomac River. The British had to march about six miles northeast of the city and cross the bridge at Bladensburg. News of this threat immediately threw the capital's 8,000 citizens into a panic!

Washingtonians ran in every direction. They loaded their belongings on wagons and poured out of the city. Many slave owners put their property in the temporary **custody** of others deep in the countryside. They didn't want their slaves to escape and find freedom with the British.

George Cockburn

Joshua Barney

General Winder put his militia in a good defensive position at the village of Bladensburg. Commodore Barney and his 500 sailors left their boats and reported for duty as **infantry**. They hauled their ship's cannons with them and placed them in the middle of General Winder's defenses. President Madison and a party of important people, including Secretary of State James Monroe, were also at Bladensburg to inspect their forces.

About noon on August 24, 1814, the British arrived and the Battle of Bladensburg began. American **artillery** thundered. The British aimed Congreve rockets at the American **lines**. When fired, these super weapons looked like giant flaming skyrockets and made shrill noises. The Congreve rocket had a shrapnel bomb attached. A shrapnel shell was designed to explode while still in the air over the enemy's heads. Then it would rain down sharp pieces of metal.

At this time in history, **antiseptics** were unknown. Even minor cuts could lead to infection and death. This made Congreve rockets deadly.

Most of the American militia lines broke when faced with the rockets. Soldiers dropped their weapons and ran toward Washington.

Some militiamen stayed to fight. These soldiers joined Commodore Barney's sailors, who made a brave stand against the British forces. Soldiers on both sides were killed. Commodore Barney was wounded and taken prisoner along with many of his troops. It was then that President Madison and his party left the battlefield and returned to Washington.

Later, British General Ross paroled Commodore Barney and his wounded men for their bravery. After removing their weapons, the injured men were sent to get medical attention.

The battle ended about four o'clock. The British forces rested at Bladensburg a few hours before moving on to Washington, D.C.

Washington Under Attack

At about eight o'clock in the evening, the British army reached the outskirts of Washington. General Ross, Admiral Cockburn, and about 100 troops entered the city carrying a flag of **truce**. They had planned on telling the citizens that they would not be harmed. But a volley of shots ripped out from a house. General Ross's horse was shot.

The British were angry and felt the rules of warfare had been violated. They killed all the people in the house and burned it down. This was the only recorded incident of British violence against civilians.

The rest of the army then began burning down the government buildings in Washington. A small group of British soldiers led by Admiral Cockburn and General Ross arrived at the President's House. They found the mansion abandoned with evidence of looting from local thieves.

British burning the President's House during the War of 1812

President's House after the British invasion, 1814

To their surprise, the soldiers found the dinner table already set for guests. They decided to sit down and enjoy their unexpected meal before setting fire to the house and its belongings.

An eyewitness reported that the President's House was quickly engulfed by fire and smoke. The hot flames completely gutted the inside and left only the four blackened walls standing. The charred walls would be used to rebuild the house after the war.

General Ross's troops stayed in Washington for about 24 hours. They set fire to the President's House, the Capitol, the Treasury Building, the Navy Yard, and several other important buildings. This was the British revenge for the American burning of the Canadian Parliament buildings at York.

Laying Down the Law

A parliament is the lawmaking body of a country. It is like the United States Congress. Representatives in parliaments or congresses make laws for the citizens of their countries.

This Washington inferno was so great that the glow in the night sky could be seen from 50 miles away. Fortunately, in the afternoon of the next day, a violent rainstorm swept over the city. It extinguished most of the flames in the public buildings.

This successful British attack on Washington, D.C, left most Americans feeling bitter and ashamed.

A SLICE OF **BLACK HISTORY**

- At the time of the attack, about 1,000 of Washington's 8,000 citizens were black slaves.
- Records show that the British invited black slaves to join their forces or be relocated in Canada or the Caribbean. These slaves would receive free passage, food, land, and freedom from slavery. The British knew the loss of slave power would weaken the American economy. Slaveholders moved their slaves away from British forces so they would have a harder time running away. Many black slaves risked their lives to find freedom with the British.
- Shortly after the War of 1812, Upper Canada's court upheld the freedom of blacks. Canada became the first place in North America where blacks were free. This led to the formation of the Underground Railroad, which helped slaves escape to Canada.
- The British invasion of Washington, D.C., prompted about 2,500 free blacks to help other Americans **fortify**, or protect, the city of Philadelphia.
- Free black sailors and slaves from the militia fought bravely in Commodore Barney's final stand against the British at Bladensburg. The black slaves hoped to be freed for their courage.
- During the British invasion of Washington, rumors of a slave rebellion spread quickly and worried many Washingtonians. The American forces kept the citizens out of the city until it was proven to be just a rumor.

Dolley and James Madison

Dolley Payne

Dolley Payne Todd Madison was born on May 20, 1768, in Hanover County, Virginia. Her parents were wealthy plantation owners. The Paynes were inspired by the speeches and pamphlets that they'd read prior to the Revolutionary War. These writings talked about the rights all people should have and the true meaning of liberty and freedom.

In a quest for a more personal truth, the Paynes became Quakers. The Quakers were a religious group that worked for human rights and were against war. In 1783, the Paynes freed their plantation slaves, sold off their lands and herds, and moved to Philadelphia. The city was the

current capital of the United States, and many Quakers lived there.

In 1790, 22-year-old Dolley Payne married Quaker lawyer John Todd. Two children were soon born. Then tragedy hit Dolley's life. In 1793, her husband and one of her children died in the yellow fever epidemic that swept the Philadelphia region. Dolley was left alone to raise her young son, Payne.

Payne Todd

Opposites Attract

About the same time that Dolley's husband and child died, her father's business failed. Her mother had to turn their 18-room family home into a boardinghouse for federal officials.

One of the boarders was Thomas Jefferson, a friend of James Madison. While visiting Jefferson at the boardinghouse, Madison became romantically interested in the widow Dolley. Later, she married this U.S. congressman. For marrying outside of her faith, Dolley was expelled from the Quaker religion.

Dolley and James were very different in personality and appearance. Dolley was taller, heavier, 17 years younger, and more outgoing than her husband. James was only five feet four inches tall and soft-spoken. In spite of these differences, they remained a loving and devoted couple.

Father of the Constitution

When James married Dolley, he was already a well-known American. Born of wealthy Virginia planters on March 16, 1751, James received an excellent education and studied law. In 1776, he became a **delegate** to the Virginia Convention. He worked closely with Thomas Jefferson to push through religious freedom laws.

The Articles of Confederation was the official document that had held the American colonies together before the Revolutionary War. After gaining independence from Great Britain, Madison felt the country needed a stronger set of rights and laws. His "Virginia Plan" became the blueprint for America's Constitution. It earned Madison the title "Father of the Constitution."

Fulfilling a promise to Thomas Jefferson, Madison later introduced the Bill of Rights. These additional rights were constitutional guarantees of civil liberties, or freedoms.

When Jefferson was elected president in 1800, he appointed Madison his secretary of state. The capital had now been moved to Washington, D.C., and Jefferson invited the Madisons to live in the President's House. During this time, Dolley often served as hostess for the widower Jefferson. When James Madison was elected president in 1808, Dolley continued to act as hostess. She also redecorated the President's House, making it more comfortable for entertaining guests.

James Madison

Fun at the White House

Dolley Madison was the first to serve ice cream in the President's House. She also planned the first inaugural ball, which is a party to celebrate a president's election. The Easter Egg Roll on the White House lawn is also one of Dolley's creations.

Portrait of Dolley Madison entertaining at the White House

Easter Egg Roll, 1921

Invasion of Washington

The British invasion of Washington was a difficult time for both Dolley and her husband. President Madison had left to check on the American defenses at Bladensburg two days earlier. Dolley was determined to stay at the President's House until he returned.

The next day, the president sent word that the British forces were stronger than expected. He instructed Dolley to pack his important cabinet papers in trunks and be ready to leave at a moment's notice.

At the same time, Secretary of State James Monroe also sent word to the State Department to secure the precious national documents. His clerks made book bags from coarse **linen**. They packed them with the original Declaration of Independence, the Constitution, and important international treaties. These documents were taken across the Potomac River to safety.

By three o'clock in the afternoon on August 24, the president hadn't returned from Bladensburg. The 100 troops assigned to guard the President's House had already fled. Still, Dolley had the dining room set with food and beverages for about 30 people. Dolley was hopeful that her husband, his cabinet, and military officers might return for a victory meal.

About that time, a horseman galloped down Pennsylvania Avenue warning everyone to leave. The British forces had defeated the American forces at Bladensburg and would march on Washington next. The messenger stopped at the President's House and reported the bad news to Dolley.

According to legend, Dolley Madison abandoned most of her own belongings and rescued Gilbert Stuart's life-sized portrait of George Washington. She had acquired the painting for the President's House at a cost of $800. Dolley told her sister in a letter that she had ordered the glass case to be broken. The picture was then cut out and given to two gentlemen friends from New York for safekeeping. They returned it to the president's wife a few weeks later.

After saving the painting, Dolley, her sister and husband, a friend of the president, and two slaves boarded her carriage. They escaped into the Virginia countryside and eventually took refuge on a farming **estate**.

East Room

Where Is It Now?

The Washington portrait that Dolley saved hangs in the East Room of the White House today.

A SLICE OF **BLACK HISTORY**

- Presidents Washington, Jefferson, and Madison all made important contributions to the cause of liberty and democracy for Americans. Yet, all three owned slaves till the end of their lives. Only George Washington provided a general **manumission** in his will. This meant that after he and his wife died, all of his 300 slaves were freed. Washington also provided for their care.

- Records show that James Madison openly acknowledged that slavery was a "great evil" but he continued to regard slaves as property. While serving as President of the United States, about 100 slaves worked on his plantation at Montpelier, Virginia.

- Paul Jennings was a slave and body servant to President James Madison. After being sold to Senator Daniel Webster and buying his freedom, Jennings wrote *A Colored Man's Reminiscences of James Madison*. In this book, he stated that his master had always shown kindness toward him. He reported that Madison hadn't allowed his plantation overseer to strike any of the slaves. Jennings also wrote that Madison had tried to keep slave families together.

- In his retirement years, James Madison served as president of the American Colonization Society. This small organization wanted a gradual emancipation of the slaves and a resettlement in a colony away from the white population. However, the majority of citizens were against this idea, so it never came to be.

- *Emancipation* means "freeing from slavery." During the Civil War, Abraham Lincoln's Emancipation Proclamation declared all slaves free. In 1865, the Thirteenth Amendment to the Constitution officially abolished slavery in the United States.

8

Fort McHenry and the Battle of New Orleans

On the night of August 25, 1814, the British ordered every Washington citizen to remain indoors from sunset to sunrise. Then the British secretly left the city. Baltimore would be their next target.

Fort McHenry

The British soldiers hated Baltimore because it was the home of the private sailing ships that had been capturing and sinking British vessels. These ships called *privateers* helped the small U.S. Navy. President Madison had issued special licenses to allow the private vessels to be armed.

The citizens in Washington, D.C., had not been ready for a British attack. But the people of Baltimore were prepared to meet the British invasion. About 13,000 regulars and militia defended the city itself. One thousand men protected Fort McHenry, which stood outside the city. **Hulks** had been sunk to help stop enemy vessels from entering the harbor.

About 3,200 militiamen held back the British land forces. Realizing they could not take Baltimore by land, the British retreated to their ships.

Then the British navy launched a heavy bombardment against Fort McHenry. Despite the heavy bombing, the fort remained in America's hands. Having failed to take Baltimore by land or water, the British left and sailed for Jamaica.

Francis Scott Key

"The Star-Spangled Banner"

An American lawyer, Francis Scott Key, was a witness to the bombardment of Fort McHenry. Thrilled by the brave defense of the fort, Key wrote a poem titled "In Defense of Fort McHenry." Set to a popular tune of the time, the poem became "The Star-Spangled Banner." Later, this song became America's national anthem.

The original Star-Spangled Banner that flew at Fort McHenry

The Battle of New Orleans

Late in November, a large British fleet carrying about 7,500 soldiers sailed to America from Jamaica. The British were under the leadership of Sir Edward Pakenham. The plan was to attack New Orleans and take control of the Mississippi River.

The troops landed in Louisiana and marched toward New Orleans. They were stopped about seven miles away by an American army under the command of Major General Andrew Jackson. Both sides suffered heavy **casualties**. Finally Jackson commanded his army to retreat and turn toward New Orleans. There, they waited for the British to arrive.

On January 8, 1815, Sir Edward Pakenham led a force of 5,300 men against Jackson's army of 4,500. Many of Jackson's men were Tennessee and Kentucky woodsmen armed with rifles.

It was a slaughter. In just a half hour, approximately 2,000 British soldiers were killed or wounded. Pakenham himself was killed. America, on the other hand, had only 71 casualties. The British retreated and sailed out to sea for good.

The Battle of New Orleans was the greatest American victory in the war. Unfortunately, it had no bearing on the outcome since the peace treaty had been signed nine days earlier. The battle did, however, give America a great leader in Andrew Jackson. His recognition and popularity helped him win the presidential election of 1828. The Battle of New Orleans also helped restore American pride.

Citizens celebrate Jackson's victory in the Battle of New Orleans.

A SLICE OF **BLACK HISTORY**

- Records show that black sailors were on board privateers that sailed out of Baltimore Harbor. They fought bravely to destroy the British shipping industry during the War of 1812.

- British forces in the Battle of New Orleans had about 1,000 black soldiers from Jamaica, Barbados, and the Bahamas. Some of these units recruited and trained American slaves who had escaped to British lines looking for freedom.

- Free black men were part of the New Orleans home guard units. They helped to protect private property and maintain order in the city. About 900 black slaves also helped fortify military positions.

- Free women of color nursed the wounded in New Orleans' hospitals.

- Before Andrew Jackson left for New Orleans, he appealed to slaves in Tennessee to join his forces in return for their freedom. Many slaves fought with him in the Battle of New Orleans, and about 50 were killed. In the end, Jackson did not grant these slaves the freedom he had promised.

- Two militia **battalions** of the "Free Men of Color" fought **with distinction** on the front lines in the Battle of New Orleans. After the battle, General Jackson told these black soldiers, "The President of the United States shall hear how praiseworthy was your conduct in the hour of danger."

- Once the black Americans were no longer needed to fight the war, promises of freedom and equality were forgotten. In the city's celebrations of the Battle of New Orleans over the next 100 years, not a single black person was allowed to participate in the festivities!

- Despite the hopes of many black slaves, the War of 1812 did not bring an end to slavery. Slavery wouldn't be abolished for another 50 years.

The Underground Railroad helped many slaves escape to freedom until slavery was finally abolished after the Civil War.

Afterword

Some historians feel that the War of 1812 with Great Britain ended in a **stalemate**. The Peace Treaty of Ghent didn't address any of America's **grievances** that had started the war. It also returned the territories captured by each side, so that no land ownership changed.

But most agree that the United States won the war in the eyes of the world. Other countries saw that Americans were willing to fight for their rights. They learned that the young democratic country would have a permanent place on the world stage.

The War of 1812 also gave birth to a mutual respect and friendship between the United States and Great Britain. This friendship grew into a strong military alliance in the 20th century.

John Rubens Smith painted this portrait representing the Treaty of Ghent. The work is entitled *Peace*.

Glossary

ale	brewed alcoholic beverage
alliance	joining of common interests among nations
antiseptic	solution that stops the growth of bacteria
artillery	weapons
barge	flat-bottomed boat used to transport goods
battalion	military troop or unit
cabinet	group of people who give advice to a leader
casualty	person killed, wounded, or lost in battle
civilian	person who is not in the military
coachman	person who drives a coach or carriage
colony	new area of land that is governed by another state or country
custody	being in charge of someone or something
delegate	representative
estate	property with a large house on it
fleet	group of warships
flintlock musket	gun with a piece of flint (stone) for striking a spark to ignite the charge
fortify	to strengthen or secure an area with forts and weapons
frigate	small warship
frontier	unsettled land on the edge of settled land
goblet	drinking glass with a stem
grievance	complaint

hulk	old ship unfit for service
infantry	soldiers trained to fight on foot
line	area where troops assemble to battle
linen	strong, lightweight cloth
looting	seizing and carrying away, especially during a war
manumission	formal freeing of slaves
maritime	relating to the sea
militia	body of citizens organized to fight in a war if necessary
mistress	female head of a household, usually one who has slaves or servants
neutral	not taking sides in a war
paroled	released (as in prisoners of war)
powder horn	container for carrying gunpowder, originally made from the horn of an ox or cow
refugee	person who flees to escape danger
regular	member of a permanent military force (as opposed to the reserves or militia)
siege	military blockade, or cutting off, of an area to force surrender
spyglass	small telescope
squadron	military unit
stalemate	situation where no one wins or benefits
tricorn	hat with three corners
truce	temporary or permanent stop in fighting
whitewash	liquid mixture used to whiten surfaces
with distinction	deserving of special honor or recognition

Index